LAKE
CHAMPLAIN

MAINE

VERMONT

NEW HAMPSHIRE

MASSACHUSETTS

NEW YORK

HUDSON RIVER

RHODE ISLAND

CONNECTICUT

NEW JERSEY

ATLANTIC OCEAN

for Bear

All rights reserved. Published by Orchard Books, an imprint of Scholastic Inc., *Publishers since 1920.*
ORCHARD BOOKS and design are registered trademarks of Watts Publishing Group, Ltd., used under license.
SCHOLASTIC and associated logos are trademarks and/or registered trademarks of Scholastic Inc.

The publisher does not have any control over and does not assume any responsibility for author or third-party websites or their content.

Library of Congress Cataloging-in-Publication Data available   ISBN 978-1-338-31226-3   10 9 8 7 6 5 4 3 2   20 21 22 23

Printed in Malaysia 108   First edition, October 2019   Book design by Elisha Cooper and Charles Kreloff

RIVER

ELISHA COOPER

ORCHARD BOOKS

NEW YORK

AN IMPRINT OF SCHOLASTIC

Morning, a mountain lake. A traveler, a canoe. As she paddles out into the blustery middle of the lake, she turns for a last wave to the shore behind her. Her journey begins.

She is alone, far from home. Gray clouds bump into the mountains above her, a hard wind blows down through the tree tops. Three hundred miles stretch in front of her. A faraway destination, a wild plan. And the question: *Can she do this?*

She takes a deep breath and pulls her paddle through the cold water.
The canoe cuts across the lake, to the headwaters of the river.

She enters the river.
Cedar trees touch
overhead, making a
green tunnel. The river is
shallow here, scraping the
canoe's underside.

She reaches into the water for a pebble
and places it in her canoe.

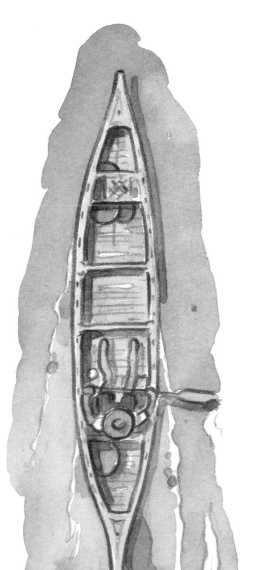

Also in her canoe: tent,
sleeping bag, guidebook, map,
life jacket, first-aid kit, waterproof
duffle with food, clothes, water
bottles, coffee pot, stove, lamp,
book, pencils, a sketchbook.

Sometimes the river is so
shallow she has to get out and
walk, pulling the canoe with a
rope like she's leading a horse.
Then the water deepens past
mossy brown rocks.

As she approaches one rock . . .

. . . the rock rises out of the river, water rippling off its back. *A moose.* The moose watches her; she watches the moose.

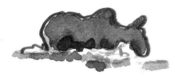

The forest is silent but for the thump of her heart and the flit-flit of the moose's ears. She floats past, keeps paddling. Around the next bend she hears thunder.

The thunder grows louder and the river rushes into a gorge, stone shelves squeezing the river tight, pushing the canoe faster and faster until the thunder is on top of them. *Rapids.*

She braces her knees against the canoe's ribs and cinches her life jacket. The river turns white and roars. Drops, jumps, leaps from pool to pool. Bashes the canoe against underwater boulders. She digs her paddle into the spray. Her hat flies off. Gone.

Her stomach flips and, for a moment, she fears the rapids will flip them over, but the canoe rights itself, and the river spits them out, down into the next rapids below.

The thunder fades with a sigh. She comes to shore. After checking to make sure the canoe is okay, she changes into long underwear and warm socks.

Hangs her bedraggled clothes to dry. Sets up her tent. Heats a bowl of soup and eats peanut butter straight from the jar, using a chocolate bar as a spoon.

Hands blistered, body sore, she writes in her sketchbook by the glow of the lamp. Above her, stars come out in the blue-black sky.

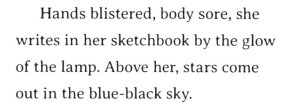

The moon climbs up among the stars. She is alone, but not. The river stays beside her, mumbling to her and to itself all through the night.

Dawn comes early, cold and sharp. She brews coffee, then breaks camp and heads downriver, sliding under an iron bridge. Rusted pickup trucks rattle above her. A driver waves. She waves back.

The river winds through the forest. New life appears around each bend: otters, ducks, dragonflies, a kingfisher. As she sketches, she wonders what word would best describe each animal. Eager otter?

She sees a blackberry bush. So she comes
to shore, and is picking berries when she hears
rustling. *A bear cub.* She stops, backs away real
slow. Floats off in the canoe.

When she camps, she plucks a flower and presses it between
pages in her sketchbook. She eats cheese and crackers. *A full
day*, she thinks. In the morning she paddles until she comes to a
stone bridge and a sign: DANGER.

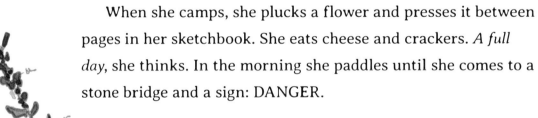

A dam. The river stops. She must portage around the dam. She takes two trips, first with her gear, then with the canoe.

She staggers — the canoe balancing on her shoulders — down the steep gravel path next to the dam. She trips, drops the canoe.

Grimacing, she checks the canoe, and her bloodied knee, then loads up and keeps paddling.

Creeks feed the river and the river widens. Cows graze in pastures at the river's side, raising their heads to watch her go. She moos at the cows; one moos back. The land hums with tractors. The air smells of cut hay.

Black flies circle her head and bite her ankles. In the evening she swims in the river and washes the day away. Treats her bruised knee, falls asleep fast. The next morning she paddles downriver until she's stopped again: a waterfall.

There's no way over the waterfall, but there is a
way around it. A lock. Locks descend the river here
like a staircase, allowing boats to navigate up or
down the river. Fishing boats and workboats wait to
enter the lock; she paddles into line. The brawny man
operating the lock bellows hello.

The operator turns a lever in his control shanty, the top gate of the lock groans open, she slides into the chamber. The operator turns another lever; water drains out of the chamber. As the water level lowers, she holds a rope to steady the canoe. Then the far gate opens, the operator bellows goodbye, and she is loosed downriver. *Onward.*

The sun hammers down and she paddles the flattened river. Sweat beads the back of her neck. The country shifts from farms with faded barns, to villages with white clapboard houses, to chimneyed factories on the outskirts of a town. At the levee she hauls up the canoe. Two boys with fishing rods watch from above.

"Where are you going?" asks the older boy. The younger boy stares wide-eyed when she tells them. It feels funny to talk. She asks them to look after her canoe and walks the streets of the old town.

It feels funny to walk. At a grocery she buys snacks, supplies, postcards, a hat. At the levee she gives the boys the snacks. The boys wish her luck.

Back in the canoe, the river feels familiar beneath her. She paddles away from town and camps that night on an island, alone again.

Where is the river? It was here last night. The river has been taken away by fog, thick and wet. So she reads in her tent, and explores the island.

High in the branches of a tree she sees a brambled nest, and down on the rocky shore, an eagle, with a fish in its talons. A striped bass, maybe a sturgeon? She opens her guidebook, then her sketchbook.

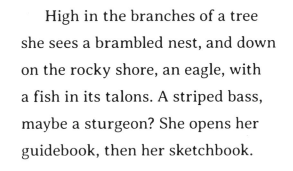

All is quiet but for the sh-sh-sh of pencil on paper. There is nothing in the world but her, the bird, this place. No one knows where she is. Then the eagle takes flight, its wings thumping the air. The morning lifts the fog away . . .

. . . and she points the nose of the canoe downriver.

Clouds roll over mountains and the river runs through the mountains, between earth and sun. The river is broad here. She hugs the shore. The land passes by, mile after mile, as she guides the canoe south past apple orchards, hilltop houses, and industrial plants.

She paddles the days and camps in the evenings. Her blisters have hardened into calluses, her sunburn turned dark. Pencils whittled down, sketchbook filling up. The days blend together. Paddling, sketching, eating, camping, paddling again. At night, when she sleeps, she dreams she is paddling under a big cloud sky.

The river snakes through craggy hills.
Rock faces loom above her and plunge
down into deep water.

She paddles with eyes narrowed, on the
lookout. Under a shadowy bridge, around
bell-ringing buoys, next to railway tracks
and a clattering freight train.

When the current is too swift, or the wind too strong, she comes to shore and waits. Writes postcards, checks her map.

Once the conditions turn she keeps going, and is paddling around a stony promontory when she senses a rumbling coming from the other side, and it's heading right at her.

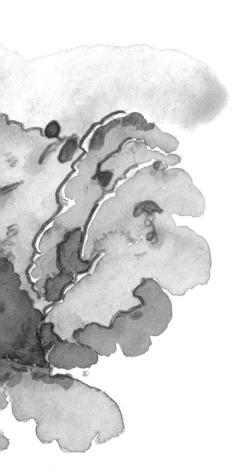

A tugboat, barreling upriver, plowing up a wake of water.
She hollers. Nobody on board sees her.

But she acts fast, turning the canoe's bow into the wake even as water crashes over the gunwale. *That was close*, she thinks.

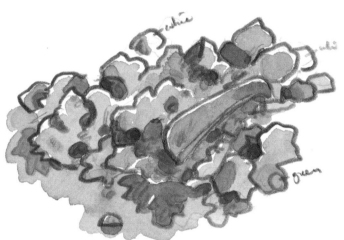

She lands, hides the canoe among a pile of rocks, walks up the main street of a village. Mails her postcards, buys a cookie at a packed bakery.

Then back to the river. As she heads out, she feels a drop of rain.

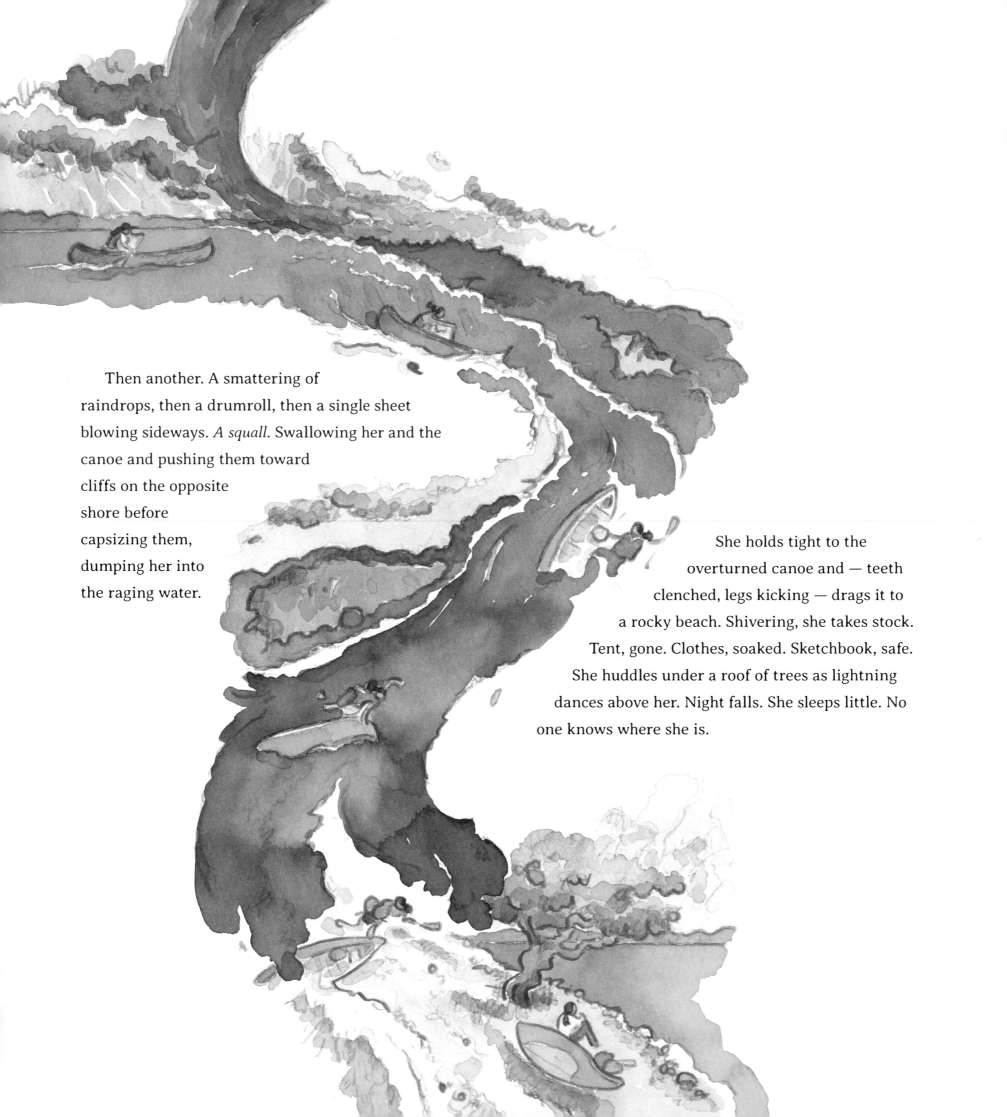

Then another. A smattering of raindrops, then a drumroll, then a single sheet blowing sideways. *A squall.* Swallowing her and the canoe and pushing them toward cliffs on the opposite shore before capsizing them, dumping her into the raging water.

She holds tight to the overturned canoe and — teeth clenched, legs kicking — drags it to a rocky beach. Shivering, she takes stock. Tent, gone. Clothes, soaked. Sketchbook, safe. She huddles under a roof of trees as lightning dances above her. Night falls. She sleeps little. No one knows where she is.

Dawn comes at last. She stretches
at the water's edge and finds a piece of
driftwood shaped like a fish.

As she paddles downriver her
body warms, then she rounds a bluff
and there's a steel suspension bridge
with arcing cables, and on the other
side of the bridge, the city.

She slips into the city, unseen. Almost unseen. A lone gull hovers above the bow of the canoe, riding the wind and watching her over its shoulder before catching a gust and rising up up up into the air, higher and higher, until the canoe is a small dark dot on the gray-blue river, one moving part in the wide world below.

Glass mountains of skyscrapers. Brick forests of buildings. Gorges of streets leading down to the river. And crisscrossing the river, boats. Scudding ferries, tacking sailboats, dueling jet skis, speeding police boats, fireboats, tour boats, tugboats shoving barges.

She paddles the length of the city and listens: growl of traffic, blare of horns, rattle of subway cars over a bridge. *A chorus.* The sounds bounce off the buildings and over ship masts and down to her. The city, old and new. She feels like an explorer. But there is someone here she knows, someone she needs to see.

She paddles through the harbor to the boatyard. Black-hulled boats and brick warehouses crowd the wharves. The air smells of diesel fuel and dirt.

Standing in front of one warehouse, beaming out at her, is a bearded man in overalls. The builder of her canoe. "How did she do?" he calls down, nodding at his handiwork. They haul the canoe to the wharf and run their hands down its sides.

They share a coffee; the builder gives her a small wrapped package. Then she launches the canoe one more time, past cranes lifting and lowering freight, out across the harbor.

Through the harbor and under a last bridge. The river stretches behind her. In front, the ocean. A hard wind blows and white clouds race overhead. The ocean is big and wild, but she is strong, and she knows what she's doing. She reads the weather and keeps the canoe steady and over the water she makes her way.

As she nears the end of her journey, she looks to the horizon and imagines the rest of the world, and a part of her wants to keep going — another adventure, another day — but closer in she sees the lighthouse, and she knows it is time for her to be home.

A seal pops its head out of the water and watches her go. Whales must be around here, too, and there is the lighthouse, rising and falling in the evening light, growing larger by the minute.

As she paddles, her mind plays forward. She can't wait to be with them again. Can't wait to tell them about moose and eagles, rapids and storms. And then to turn her sketches into paintings and her words into a story.

Now she sees them. Her family. Her children waving, her dog racing down the sand. So she paddles harder, as hard as she can . . .

. . . and brings the canoe to shore.

Author's Note

I did not canoe down the Hudson River. I am not a capable enough canoer.
Or a brave enough one. Especially that last stretch where New York Harbor merges into
the Atlantic Ocean, with its treacherous currents and tides and boat traffic. But an experienced
traveler could make this trip. A few have. It would take considerable planning, stamina and heart, and about twenty days.

To research this book, I drove alongside the Hudson. Overnight trips into the Adirondacks to explore the river's upper reaches, day trips
from New York City, during which I crossed countless bridges in search of the right view. To feel water beneath me, I kayaked down the
Batten Kill River in upstate New York, a sketchbook on my lap. And I paddled around a lake in northern Maine in a Rangeley Lakes boat —
wood-ribbed, black-sided, red-striped. It belonged to my grandfather, and now belongs to me.

My thanks to the Sendak Fellowship; its farm in upstate New York provided the perfect space to launch this book. Thanks to Brian Floca
for our talks. Thanks to Ken Geist and David Saylor. Also to Bianca Calabresi, Rebecca Schosha, Paul Greenberg, Janice Nimura, Sacha
Spector, Barney Latimer, Toby Cox, and Elise Cappella. Thanks to my daughters, Zoë and Mia, who were excellent canoer models.

A Note on the Hudson River

It was called *Cahohatatea* ("The River") by the Iroquois who canoed it, *Noortrivier* ("North River") by the Dutch who sailed it, and finally the Hudson River, for Henry Hudson, the English explorer who navigated up the river in 1609. He failed in his search for a northwest passage but succeeded in having a great river named after him.

The Hudson begins in the wilderness of Adirondack Park and ends three hundred and fifteen miles later in the harbor of New York City. The river's source is tiny Lake Tear of the Clouds; it becomes navigable in the clear blue waters of Henderson Lake, where our traveler starts her journey.

The Adirondack Park is huge. Almost six million acres of mountain peaks and sweeping forest, the perfect habitat to black bears, waterfowl, deer, and moose. Winslow Homer, the nineteenth-century artist, painted beautiful watercolors of the Adirondack's wildlife. Its abundant lakes, bogs, wetlands, and streams feed into the Hudson as it winds its way south.

Then the river turns east, entering the Hudson Gorge and a stretch of difficult rapids. After passing under a red bridge in the town of Riparius, the river bends back through the mill towns of Glens Falls and Hudson Falls. Dams force travelers to carry, or portage, their canoes. Locks allow boaters to get around waterfalls — like the ones that would have stopped Henry Hudson. Locks also link the river north to Lake Champlain and Canada, and west to the Great Lakes by way of the Erie Canal.

The Erie Canal, completed in 1825, connected the middle of the country to New York. America expanded. More change followed: railroads, industry, pollution. Companies dumped their waste in the river, decimating its population of sturgeon, striped bass, and shad. Pete Seeger, the singer and activist, spurred a movement for clean water laws. In recent years the river has begun to return to health. Eagles now nest alongside the Hudson.

After the town of Troy, the river becomes tidal. The tides of the Atlantic push north into the river, against its flow (Mohicans called it *Muhheakantuck*, or "The River that Flows Both Ways"). The Catskill Mountains rise to the west. The dramatic landscape inspired the Hudson River School, a nineteenth-century group of artists. Their paintings of the valley were thought to be overly romantic; maybe they were just accurate. One painter, Frederic Church, built his home overlooking the river because of the view.

After running straight south, the Hudson twists around Storm King and Bear Mountain. The mountains here look to me like Scylla and Charybdis, the mythic monsters from the *Odyssey* that threaten to destroy boats that pass between them. (Any story of a long trip home by boat owes something to Homer's *Odyssey*).

Forts built during the Revolutionary War took advantage of this forbidding topography; a chain was even strung across the river to stop British boats. The Hudson was strategically important — whoever controlled the river controlled the country. Benedict Arnold fled across it. George Washington, after losing the Battle of Brooklyn, crossed the river with his army near where the George Washington Bridge now stands, retreating to fight another day.

As the Hudson enters New York Harbor it passes the island of Manhattan (*Mannahatta*, or "The Island of Many Hills" to the Lenape). Imagine this island as it once was. Wild and forested, its waters teeming with shorebirds, fish, oysters, and whales. A perfect port, deep and protected. The early Dutch recognized this, settling on the island's southern tip. Then the English took over, and the town grew into a port bristling with masts, then smokestacks, then skyscrapers. Across from Manhattan, the Brooklyn Navy Yard built battleships for World War II; today it is home to artisans like those who could have built our traveler's canoe.

Container ships now head out from New York Harbor under the Verrazano Bridge to distant ports, passing the lighthouse at Sandy Hook — the oldest standing lighthouse in the United States — where our traveler ends her journey.

Think of the great cities of the world. Chances are they're on an ocean, or a river. London, Shanghai, New York. Humans are bound to water. Our history tied to exploration, trade, and boats. We navigate between the countryside and the city, and then to other countries. We are connected by water, more connected to each other than we know.

Sometimes, when I'm feeling low or uninspired, I go down to the Hudson near where I live in Manhattan and I look at the river flow past. I imagine how the water I am looking at was once in a clear blue lake upstate — and maybe someone there is looking at the water, too — and knowing this fills me with wonder.

Sources & Reading

Benjamin, Vernon. *The History of the Hudson River Valley: from Wilderness to the Civil War.* New York: The Overlook Press, 2014.

Benjamin, Vernon. *The History of the Hudson River Valley: from the Civil War to Modern Times.* New York: The Overlook Press, 2016.

Bruce, Wallace. *Panorama of the Hudson: Showing Both Sides of the River from New York to Albany.* New York: Bryant Literary Union, 1888.

Holling, Holling Clancy. *Paddle-to-the-Sea.* Boston: Houghton Mifflin Company, 1941.

Homer. *The Odyssey.* Translated by E.V. Rieu. Revised translation by D.C.H. Rieu. New York: Penguin Books, 2013.

Lourie, Peter. *River of Mountains: A Canoe Journey down the Hudson.* Syracuse: Syracuse University Press, 1995.

Maclean, Norman. *A River Runs Through It: And Other Stories.* Chicago: The University of Chicago Press, 1976.

Manley, Atwood. *Rushton and His Times in American Canoeing.* Syracuse: Syracuse University Press, 1968.

"Map of Hudson's River, with the adjacent country." *The New York Public Library Digital Collections.*

Shorto, Russell. *The Island at the Center of the World: The Epic Story of Dutch Manhattan & The Forgotten Colony That Shaped America.* New York: Doubleday, 2004.

Tatham, David. *Winslow Homer in the Adirondacks.* Syracuse: Syracuse University Press, 1996.

Twain, Mark. *Adventures of Huckleberry Finn.* New York: Penguin Books, 2014.

Whitman, Walt. *Leaves of Grass.* New York: Penguin Books, 1986.

Henderson Lake

Adirondack Park

LAKE CHAMPLAIN

moose

Hudson Gorge

campsite

bear

Glens Falls Dam

VERMONT

NEW HAMPSHIRE

LAKE ONTARIO

lock

Troy

Catskill Mountains

eagle

MASSACH

NEW YORK

H U D S O N   R I V E R

Hudson River Valley

CONNECTICUT

RHODE ISLAND

Bear Mountain

tugboat

squall

PENNSYLVANIA

George Washington Bridge

Manhattan

NEW JERSEY

Brooklyn Navy Yard

Sandy Hook Lighthouse

New York City Harbor